I Love You Mummy

Catherine
Vāse

For Becca –
the Queen of Styles,
Jonny-fun,
Milla Moo and
Zaccy boy
C.V.

Mummy, if you were something
I could put on every day,

you would be a woolly jumper,
soft and snug.

If you were a place,
you would be a summer meadow,

golden sunshine
falling on my face.

If you were a bird,
singing in a tree,

you would sing
**your special
song just for me.**

If you were a fruit,
you would be a juicy strawberry,

sweet and red . . .
my favourite treat!

If you were a sound, you'd be
a cat's gentle purr,

as I tickle its soft, furry head.

And, Mummy, if you were
something bright . . .

you'd be the moon
**watching over
me at night.**

But you are all of these things,
because you are you.

You are my mummy and
I love you.

And if you were a book,
I would turn you upside down
and read some more!

And if you were a book,
I would turn you upside down
and read some more!

You are my daddy and
I love you.

But you are
all of these things,
because you are
you...

And, Daddy,
if you were
something bright,

you'd be the North Star
watching over
me at night.

If you were a noise,
you would be as
loud as a drum,

**Boom! Bang!
Bang!**

And just as cool!

silly as a belly flop,

splish! splash! **splosh!**

into a pool.

If you were a joke, you'd be as . . .

If you were a meal, you'd be
a big bowl of spaghetti,

twisty, twirly and very,
very messy!

If you were a toy, you would be
a roaring lion,

with a long, swishing tail and golden mane.

Daddy, if you were something
I could put upon my feet,

you would be a pair of wellies for
splashing in the rain.

I Love You Daddy!

Catherine
Vāse

First published in
Great Britain in 2010 by
Gullane Children's Books
This edition published in 2011 by
Gullane Children's Books
185 Fleet Street,
London, EC4A 2HS
www.gullanebooks.com

10 9 8 7 6 5 4 3 2 1

Text and illustrations
© Catherine Vāse 2010

The right of Catherine Vāse
to be identified as the author
and illustrator of this work
has been asserted by her in
accordance with the Copyright,
Designs and Patents Act, 1988.
A CIP record for this title is
available from the British Library.

ISBN: 978-1-86233-859-3

Printed and bound in China

GULLANE
CHILDREN'S BOOKS